Willow's Whispers

To Jane, Jordan and Carlyn. Thanks for years of support,
suggestions and encouragement! — L.B.

For my husband, Paul, who always hears my whispers — T.H.

Text © 2010 Lana Button
Illustrations © 2010 Tania Howells

Kids Can Press acknowledges the financial support
of the Government of Ontario, through the Ontario Media
Development Corporation's Ontario Book Initiative; the
Ontario Arts Council; the Canada Council for the Arts; and
the Government of Canada, through the BPIDP, for our
publishing activity.

Published in Canada by   Published in the U.S. by
Kids Can Press Ltd.   Kids Can Press Ltd.
25 Dockside Drive   2250 Military Road
Toronto, ON M5A 0B5   Tonawanda, NY 14150

www.kidscanpress.com

Kids Can Press is a *Corus*™ Entertainment company

The artwork in this book was rendered in Photoshop.
The text is set in Univers 45 and Berthold Bodoni.

Edited by Yvette Ghione
Designed by Karen Powers

This book is smyth sewn casebound.
Manufactured in Shenzhen, Guang Dong, P.R. China, in 2/2011
by Printplus Limited

CM 10 0 9 8 7 6 5 4 3

Library and Archives Canada Cataloguing in Publication

Button, Lana, 1968 —
    Willow's whispers / written by Lana Button ;
illustrated by Tania Howells.

ISBN 978-1-55453-280-3

I. Howells, Tania II. Title.

PS8603.U87W54 2010   jC813'.6   C2009-903897-8

Willow's Whispers

Written by **Lana Button** Illustrated by **Tania Howells**

KIDS CAN PRESS

Willow's words came out in whispers.

They were just too tiny to hear.

She wished they would come out so loud
and clear that everyone would notice!

But when Willow spoke, her words slipped out

as soft

and shy

as a secret.

I'm Willow.

At school, when Jane and Julian made room
at their table and asked, "Want to sit here?"

Willow whispered,

"I'd love to."

"Oh, well," said Jane. Julian shrugged.

"She must like sitting alone."

Willow's shoulders sank.

No one heard her reply,

"No, I don't."

At snack time, when Mrs. Post asked,
"Would you like apple juice or orange juice?"
Willow whispered, "Apple, please."
"Pardon me, dear?" asked Mrs. Post.
"Apple, please," Willow tried again.

Mrs. Post smiled and poured her orange juice.
"There you go, dear."

Willow sighed. She drank it anyway,
even though it made her lip crinkle.

At playtime, when Willow gathered
the dollhouse family for a picnic
and Kristabelle snatched away
the baby, Willow whispered,
"I'm playing with her."
   "Excuse me?"
sneered Kristabelle.
   "I'm playing with her,"
Willow repeated.

But Kristabelle just skipped away.
Willow said nothing.
She had the picnic anyway,
even though the dolls had
lost their appetites.

At the end of the day, Mrs. Post said,
"Those of you who have not had a turn
to be Line Leader, please speak up."
Willow whispered, "I haven't had a turn."
"Anyone?" asked Mrs. Post.

"I haven't."

So Mrs. Post chose Kristabelle as Line Leader. *Again.*
Willow scuffed her feet to her usual spot, at the end of the line.

Even at bedtime, when Willow's
dad tucked her in and said good night,
Willow whispered,

"Good night."

But Dad was an expert at
hearing Willow's whispers.

He never said "What?"
or "Pardon?" or "Who?"

He just wrapped Willow tight
in a big bear hug and whispered
right back, "Your big, strong voice
got stuck way inside you, Willow.
That happens sometimes.
But one day your voice will
wiggle its way out."

doll apple juice

picnic play big unstuck

surprise Julian loud

magic I wish ... lucky

strong star

wiggle Jane

Line Leader happy

Willow lay awake that night, searching for a way to make **louder** words.

She wished and thought and planned until she fell asleep.

The next morning, Willow jumped out
of bed and headed for the recycling bin.
She rooted and rummaged until she
found just the thing.

Then she gathered
markers and glitter
and glue and rushed
to her room.

When Willow finally
came out, she was holding a
magic microphone!

That day at school, Willow pressed the magic microphone
to her lips and told Jane and Julian,

"I'd love to sit with you."

"Great!" said Jane as she and Julian
scooted over. "You can share our crayons."
Willow could hardly believe her ears!

At snack time, when Mrs. Post asked,
"Would you like apple juice or orange juice?"
Willow said,

"Apple, please."

"There you go, dear," Mrs. Post said.
Willow drank her juice in one gulp.
Her lip didn't crinkle a bit.

At playtime, when Kristabelle tried to snatch away the dollhouse baby, Willow trumpeted,

"I'm playing with her."

Not only did Kristabelle hear Willow, **the whole class heard her!**

It was a perfect day for a picnic.
The dolls had two helpings of everything.

But at the end of the day, when Mrs. Post said, "Those of you who have not had a turn to be Line Leader, please speak up," the microphone slipped from Willow's hand.

First there was a **thunk,** and then a horrible **scrunch.**

Willow picked up the crumpled
cardboard tube and tried,
"I haven't had a turn."
"Anyone?" asked Mrs. Post.

Something was stirring way
inside Willow. It twisted. It turned.
It wiggled its way out!

She put down the crumpled tube,
took a brave breath and with her
own big, strong voice, said,

And everyone (even Kristabelle) cheered as Willow the Line Leader led the class out the door.